Tommy
And The Wonder
Of Wildlife

Inspirational Short Stories for Kids 9-12

Tommy and the Wonder of Wildlife is an inspiring collection of short stories for kids ages 9-12. Written in a captivating and easy-to-read style, this book takes readers on a journey through the natural world, introducing them to a wide variety of animals and their important role in the ecosystem.

Each of the 10 stories in the book focuses on a different creature. Through the adventures of the book's main character, Tommy, children will learn about the importance of conservation, the beauty of nature, and the interconnectedness of all living things.

Tommy and the Wonder of Wildlife is a book perfect for children who love to learn about Animals, wildlife, and the natural world.

Copyright © 2023

Lorraine Buller

CONTENTS PAGE

1 - Tommy and the Brave Little Squirrel

Once upon a time, in a small town nestled in the woods, there lived a young boy named Tommy. Tommy was an adventurous and curious child who loved to explore the forest behind his house. One day, while exploring the woods, Tommy stumbled upon a small squirrel who had fallen out of its nest. The little squirrel was shivering and scared, and Tommy knew he had to help it.

Tommy carefully picked up the squirrel and brought it back to his house. He made a small bed for it in a box, and put a warm blanket inside. He found some nuts and seeds in his kitchen and made a small meal for the squirrel. The squirrel ate hungrily and soon fell asleep.

The next morning, Tommy woke up early to check on the squirrel. To his surprise, the squirrel was gone. He searched his room and the rest of his house, but the squirrel was nowhere to be found. Disappointed, Tommy went outside to explore the woods again. As he was walking, he heard a rustling in the bushes. He cautiously approached, and to his delight, the squirrel appeared from behind the bushes.

The squirrel ran to Tommy and climbed up his leg, chattering away excitedly. Tommy laughed and picked up the squirrel, holding it close. The squirrel nuzzled into his neck and seemed to be trying to say thank you. From that day on, the squirrel and Tommy were the best of friends. They would spend hours together, exploring the woods and finding new things to see and do.

Tommy realized that the squirrel had taught him an important lesson: No matter how small or weak you may feel, with a little help and care, you can do great things. From that day on, Tommy made it his mission to help and protect all the animals he met. He became an advocate for wildlife conservation, and eventually, he grew up to become a wildlife biologist, dedicating his life to protect and conserve the wildlife.

The story of Tommy and the brave little squirrel spread throughout the town, and it became a legend among the children. They would often go to the woods in search of the brave little squirrel, hoping to catch a glimpse of it, and learn the same lesson that Tommy learned. And so, the memory of Tommy and the brave little squirrel lived on, inspiring generations of children to be kind, compassionate and to protect the nature.

2 - The Friendship of Tommy and the Fawn

Tommy was walking through the forest one day when he stumbled upon a young fawn. The fawn was lying on the ground, and it seemed to be injured. Tommy knew he had to help, so he carefully picked up the fawn and brought it back to his house.

Once he arrived home, he immediately called the local wildlife rescue center, and they instructed him on how to take care of the fawn until they could come to pick it up. He cleaned and bandaged the fawn's wounds and made sure it was comfortable and warm.

As the days went by, Tommy and the fawn grew very close. The fawn followed him everywhere and even slept by his side at night. Tommy named the fawn Bambi, and he was determined to help her recover. He would spend hours sitting with her, talking to her and keeping her company.

One day, the wildlife rescue center called to say that Bambi was ready to be released back into the wild. Tommy was sad to see her go, but he knew it was for the best. He took Bambi to a nearby meadow, where he said goodbye. Bambi looked at Tommy with her big brown eyes and nuzzled him, as if to say thank you.

Tommy watched as Bambi ran off into the meadow, rejoining her family. He felt a sense of happiness and sadness at the same time. He was happy that Bambi was back where she belonged, but he would miss her dearly.

As he walked back home, he realized that the experience had taught him a valuable lesson. He learned that friendships can come in unexpected ways and that they can be just as strong and meaningful regardless of the time they last. He also learned that sometimes, letting go of something you love is necessary for their well-being and happiness.

From that day on, Tommy became a friend of the animals, always willing to help and protect them. He would often go back to the meadow, hoping to catch a glimpse of Bambi and her family, and whenever he did, his heart would fill with joy and gratitude for the friendship they shared.

The story of Tommy and Bambi, the young fawn, spread throughout the town, and it became a legend among the children. They would often go to the meadow in search of Bambi, hoping to catch a glimpse of her, and learn the same lesson that Tommy learned. And so, the memory of Tommy and Bambi lived on, inspiring generations of children to be kind, compassionate and to protect the nature.

3 - Tommy and the Wise Old Owl

One night, while camping in the woods with his family, Tommy heard a strange hooting noise. He couldn't sleep, so he decided to go investigate. He walked deeper into the woods and soon came upon a large owl perched on a tree branch. The owl was staring at him with its big, round eyes, and Tommy couldn't help but feel a sense of awe and wonder.

He slowly approached the owl, and to his surprise, the owl didn't fly away. Instead, it let out a soft hoot and seemed to be trying to communicate with him. Tommy was intrigued and decided to stay and listen. As he listened to the owl's hoots, he felt like he could understand what the owl was saying.

The owl told him that there was a nearby tree that had been struck by lightning, and it was causing a fire that was spreading quickly. The owl asked for Tommy's help to put out the fire before it reached the nearby forest. Without hesitation, Tommy ran back to camp, woke up his family and told them about the fire. Together, they put out the fire and saved the forest.

The next morning, as they were packing up camp, Tommy went back to the owl to thank it for alerting him to the fire. The owl was nowhere to be found, but Tommy felt a sense of gratitude and connection to the wise old owl.

From that day on, Tommy had a new appreciation for the beauty and wisdom of nature. He began to study owls and other birds of prey, and eventually became an ornithologist. He dedicated his life to protecting and conserving these magnificent creatures.

The story of Tommy and the wise old owl spread throughout the town, and it became a legend among the children. They would often go to the woods in search of the wise old owl, hoping to catch a glimpse of it, and learn the same lesson that Tommy learned. And so, the memory of Tommy and the wise old owl lived on, inspiring generations of children to be kind, compassionate and to protect the nature.

4 - The Adventure of Tommy and the Lost Dolphin

One day, while swimming in the ocean, Tommy saw something moving in the water far off in the distance. He swam towards it and soon realized it was a dolphin. But this was not an ordinary dolphin, it had a large gash on its side and it seemed to be lost and disoriented.

Tommy knew he had to help, so he swam closer to the dolphin and tried to comfort it. The dolphin seemed to trust him and allowed him to help it. He helped the dolphin back to the shore and called the marine rescue center for help.

The rescue center arrived soon after and took the dolphin to their facility for treatment. Tommy was sad to see the dolphin go, but he knew it was for the best. He visited the dolphin every day at the rescue center, and they grew a strong bond.

The dolphin's injury was serious and it would take a long time for it to recover. Tommy knew he had to do something to help. He started raising money for the rescue center and organizing beach cleanups to help protect marine life.

Months passed, and the dolphin's health improved. The rescue center decided it was time to release the dolphin back into the wild. Tommy was excited but also sad to say goodbye to his new friend. The day of the release came, and Tommy was there to see the dolphin set free.

As the dolphin swam out to sea, it turned around and looked at Tommy. It let out a joyful cry and then dove under the water. Tommy felt a lump in his throat and a tear rolled down his cheek. He knew that the dolphin would always hold a special place in his heart.

From that day on, Tommy became an advocate for marine conservation. He dedicated his life to protecting and preserving the ocean and its inhabitants. He would often go back to the beach where he rescued the dolphin, hoping to catch a glimpse of it, and whenever he did, his heart would fill with joy and gratitude for the adventure they shared.

The story of Tommy and the lost dolphin spread throughout the town, and it became a legend among the children. They would often go to the beach in search of the lost dolphin, hoping to catch a glimpse of it, and learn the same lesson that Tommy learned. And so, the memory of Tommy and the lost dolphin lived on, inspiring generations of children to be kind, compassionate and to protect the nature.

5 - Tommy and the Secret of the Butterfly Garden

One day, while exploring the woods, Tommy came across a beautiful garden filled with colorful butterflies. He had never seen anything like it before. The butterflies were fluttering around, and it was a sight to behold.

As he walked through the garden, he noticed that there was a small sign that read "Butterfly Sanctuary - Keep Out" He wondered why the garden was off-limits and decided to investigate further.

He soon discovered that the garden was being used as a sanctuary for endangered butterflies. The butterflies were being bred and protected in the garden so that their population could recover. Tommy realized how important this sanctuary was and how much he wanted to help.

He started volunteering at the sanctuary, helping to care for the butterflies. He learned how to feed them, create habitats, and release them back into the wild. He loved every moment spent in the garden and felt a sense of purpose and fulfillment.

As he was working at the sanctuary, he discovered that the garden was in danger. The land was being sold to developers, and if the garden was destroyed, the butterflies would have nowhere to go. Tommy knew he had to do something to save the garden.

He rallied the community and began a campaign to save the butterfly sanctuary. He organized rallies, wrote letters, and made speeches. His efforts paid off, and the garden was saved.

The story of Tommy and the secret butterfly garden spread throughout the town, and it became a legend among the children. They would often go to the garden in search of butterflies, hoping to catch a glimpse of them, and learn the same lesson that Tommy learned. And so, the memory of Tommy and the secret butterfly garden lived on, inspiring generations of children to be kind, compassionate and to protect the nature.

From that day on, Tommy became an advocate for conservation and environmental issues. He dedicated his life to protecting and preserving endangered species and their habitats. He would often go back to the butterfly sanctuary, hoping to catch a glimpse of the colorful butterflies, and whenever he did, his heart would fill with joy and gratitude for the secret garden that changed his life.

6 - The Courage of Tommy and the Grizzly Bear

One day, while exploring the woods, Tommy came across a grizzly bear. The bear was massive, and Tommy knew he had to be careful. He slowly backed away, but the bear didn't seem to be aggressive. It was just foraging for food.

Tommy was curious and wanted to get a closer look. He slowly walked towards the bear, and to his surprise, the bear let him get closer. Tommy felt a sense of awe and wonder as he looked into the bear's eyes. He realized that the bear was just like him, trying to survive and provide for its family.

As he was observing the bear, he noticed that it seemed to be struggling to find food. The bear's usual food source, the berries, were scarce that year and the bear was malnourished. Tommy knew he had to do something to help.

He began to bring food to the bear every day, leaving it near the bear's den. The bear grew to trust Tommy and would come to him when it was hungry. Tommy felt a strong connection to the bear, and he knew he had to help it in any way he could.

As the days passed, the bear's health improved, and it started to look more like a healthy grizzly bear. But Tommy knew that the bear's future was still uncertain. He knew that the bear would have to be released back into the wild soon, and he worried about what would happen to it.

Tommy decided to start educating the local community about the importance of bears and how to coexist with them. He organized events, gave speeches, and made videos to raise awareness about the grizzly bears and the importance of preserving their habitats.

Eventually, the bear was released back into the wild, and Tommy felt a mix of sadness and happiness. He was happy that the bear was back where it belonged, but he would miss it dearly.

The story of Tommy and the courage of the grizzly bear spread throughout the town, and it became a legend among the children. They would often go to the woods in search of the bear, hoping to catch a glimpse of it, and learn the same lesson that Tommy learned. And so, the memory of Tommy and the grizzly bear lived on, inspiring generations of children to be kind, compassionate, and to protect the nature.

From that day on, Tommy became an advocate for wildlife conservation, and he dedicated his life to protecting and preserving habitats and species, especially the grizzly bears. He would often go back to the woods, hoping to catch a glimpse of the bear, and whenever he did, his heart would fill with joy and gratitude for the courage of the grizzly bear that changed his life.

7 - Tommy and the Mysterious Sea Turtles

One day, while walking on the beach, Tommy came across a group of sea turtles. They were crawling out of the ocean and making their way to the dunes to lay their eggs. He had never seen anything like it before, and he was fascinated.

As he watched the sea turtles, he noticed that they seemed to be struggling. The beach was crowded, and people were stepping on their nests and blocking their path. Tommy knew he had to do something to help.

He started to educate the local community about the sea turtles and the importance of their nesting sites. He organized beach cleanups, set up barriers around the nests, and made signs to raise awareness.

As the sea turtle nesting season progressed, Tommy saw that more and more sea turtles were successfully laying their eggs and returning to the ocean. He was thrilled to see the positive impact of his efforts.

One night, as Tommy was walking on the beach, he saw a sea turtle hatchling making its way to the ocean. It was a small, fragile creature, and Tommy knew it faced many challenges on its journey. He decided to follow it and make sure it reached the ocean safely.

As he followed the hatchling, he encountered obstacles such as trash and debris on the beach, lights from nearby buildings that disoriented the hatchling, and even people who didn't understand the importance of the sea turtles. Tommy had to act quickly and make sure the hatchling reached the ocean safely.

He eventually reached the water's edge with the hatchling, and he watched as it swam out to sea. He felt a sense of joy and accomplishment. He knew that the sea turtle would have a better chance of survival thanks to his efforts.

The story of Tommy and the mysterious sea turtles spread throughout the town, and it became a legend among the children. They would often go to the beach in search of sea turtles, hoping to catch a glimpse of them, and learn the same lesson that Tommy learned. And so, the memory of Tommy and the sea turtles lived on, inspiring generations of children to be kind, compassionate, and to protect the nature.

From that day on, Tommy became an advocate for marine conservation, and he dedicated his life to protecting and preserving marine life, especially the sea turtles. He would often go back to the beach, hoping to catch a glimpse of sea turtles, and whenever he did, his heart would fill with joy and gratitude for the mysterious sea turtles that changed his life.

8 - The Inspiration of Tommy and the Bald Eagle

One day, while exploring the woods, Tommy came across a majestic bald eagle. It was perched on a tree branch, surveying its surroundings. Tommy was in awe of the powerful and beautiful bird.

As he watched the eagle, he noticed that it seemed to be struggling. Its nest was in disrepair, and it seemed that it wouldn't be able to raise its young. Tommy knew he had to do something to help.

He decided to repair the eagle's nest. He gathered branches and twigs from the woods and set to work. He worked tirelessly, and soon the nest was complete.

The eagle was hesitant at first, but soon it warmed up to the new nest and made it its home. Tommy felt a sense of satisfaction and joy as he saw the eagle raising its young in the nest.

As he was leaving the eagle in its new nest, he noticed that the surrounding forest was being cut down for logging. He knew that the destruction of the forest would not only displace the eagle but also many other animals that call it home.

Tommy rallied the community and began a campaign to save the forest. He organized rallies, wrote letters, and made speeches to raise awareness about the importance of preserving the forest and the wildlife that lived there.

Thanks to Tommy's efforts, the forest was saved, and the eagle was able to raise its young in a safe and stable environment.

The story of Tommy and the bald eagle spread throughout the town, and it became a legend among the children. They would often go to the woods in search of the eagle, hoping to catch a glimpse of it, and learn the same lesson that Tommy learned. And so, the memory of Tommy and the bald eagle lived on, inspiring generations of children to be kind, compassionate, and to protect the nature.

From that day on, Tommy became an advocate for conservation and environmental issues. He dedicated his life to protecting and preserving natural habitats, especially for the bald eagle and other wildlife. He would often go back to the woods, hoping to catch a glimpse of the bald eagle, and whenever he did, his heart would fill with joy and gratitude for the inspiration of the bald eagle that changed his life.

Tommy's actions not only saved the bald eagle and its family, but also many other animals and plants that call the forest home. He showed how one person's actions can make a positive impact on the environment and the lives of animals. He became a role model for many children and adults in the community and his legacy of conservation and protection of nature lived on.

9 - Tommy and the Wonder of the Whales

One day, while swimming in the ocean, Tommy saw something moving in the water far off in the distance. He swam towards it and soon realized it was a pod of whales. They were majestic creatures, and Tommy couldn't help but feel a sense of awe and wonder.

He swam closer to the whales and watched as they gracefully swam and dove in the ocean. He noticed that they seemed to be communicating with each other and he was fascinated by their intelligence and social behavior.

As he was observing the whales, he noticed that they seemed to be struggling. Pollution and overfishing were damaging their habitats and reducing their food sources. Tommy knew he had to do something to help.

He started educating the local community about the importance of whales and the impact of human activities on their habitats. He organized beach cleanups and campaigns to reduce pollution, and he encouraged sustainable fishing practices.

As he was working to protect the whales, he had the opportunity to go on a whale watching tour. He was thrilled to be able to see the whales up close and learn more about them. On the tour, he was surprised to see a whale with a large fishing net entangled in its tail. He knew that the whale would not survive if the net wasn't removed.

Without hesitation, he jumped into the water and swam towards the whale. He carefully cut the net from the whale's tail, and the whale was finally free. The whale seemed to thank him by swimming around him for a moment before diving back into the ocean.

From that day on, Tommy became an advocate for marine conservation and he dedicated his life to protecting and preserving the ocean and its inhabitants, especially the whales. He would often go back to the ocean, hoping to catch a glimpse of the magnificent creatures, and whenever he did, his heart would fill with joy and gratitude for the wonder of the whales that changed his life.

The story of Tommy and the wonder of the whales spread throughout the town, and it became a legend among the children. They would often go to the ocean in search of the whales, hoping to catch a glimpse of them, and learn the same lesson that Tommy learned. And so, the memory of Tommy and the wonder of the whales lived on, inspiring generations of children to be kind, compassionate, and to protect the nature.

10 - The Lesson of Tommy and the Endangered Panda

One day, while exploring a zoo, Tommy came across a giant panda. It was a majestic and gentle creature, and Tommy couldn't help but feel a sense of awe and wonder. He was fascinated by the panda's distinctive black and white markings and its peaceful demeanor.

As he watched the panda, he learned that it was an endangered species and that there were very few left in the wild. He was saddened by this news and wanted to learn more about the panda and what he could do to help.

He began to research the panda and learned about the challenges it faced in the wild, such as habitat loss and poaching. He also learned about the conservation efforts being made to protect the panda and its habitat.

Tommy was inspired to take action and help the panda. He started volunteering at the zoo, helping to care for the panda and educating visitors about its conservation. He also started a fundraising campaign to support conservation efforts in the panda's native China.

Through his efforts, Tommy was able to raise awareness and funds for panda conservation. He also was able to educate many people about the importance of protecting endangered species and preserving their habitats.

As he was leaving the zoo after one of his volunteer shifts, he saw a group of people illegally buying and selling panda pelts. He knew that this was a major contributor to the panda's decline in the wild. He confronted the poachers and reported them to the authorities.

Thanks to Tommy's actions, the poachers were caught and the panda pelts were seized. He also made sure that the poachers were educated about the importance of protecting endangered species and the consequences of their actions.

From that day on, Tommy became an advocate for endangered species conservation and habitat preservation. He dedicated his life to raising awareness and funds for conservation efforts, and he became known as the "panda protector" in the community. He would often go back to the zoo to check on the panda and make sure it was well cared for.

He also started educating the local community about the importance of protecting endangered species and preserving their habitats. He organized events and gave talks to schools and community groups, spreading awareness and encouraging people to be mindful of the impact they have on the environment.

The panda became a symbol of hope and resilience in the community, and it was a reminder of the impact that one person can have on the environment and the lives of animals. Thanks to Tommy's efforts, the panda was able to live in a safe and stable environment and inspire others to take action and protect endangered species.

Printed in Great Britain
by Amazon